Storyteller Tales

The Generous Rabbit
and other animal stori

What happened to the kind rabbit? How did the sparrow beat the crocodile? And what happened to the curious frog?

Find out in this book of traditional stories from around the world. These imaginative retellings bring animals of all kinds vividly to life and are full of action and fun.

Bob Hartman is a widely acclaimed author and storyteller. He is best known for *The Lion Storyteller Bible* and other books in the *Storyteller* series in which these tales were originally published.

The Generous Rabbit

and other animal stories

Bob Hartman

Illustrations by
Brett Hudson

LION
CHILDREN'S

Text copyright © 1998 and 2002 Bob Hartman
Illustrations copyright © 2004 Brett Hudson of GCI
This edition copyright © 2004 Lion Hudson

The moral rights of the author and illustrator
have been asserted

A Lion Children's Book
an imprint of
Lion Hudson plc
Mayfield House, 256 Banbury Road,
Oxford OX2 7DH, England
www.lionhudson.com
ISBN-13: 978-0-7459-4697-9
ISBN-10: 0-7459-4697-6

First edition 2004
10 9 8 7 6 5 4 3 2 1

Acknowledgments
These stories were first published in *The Lion
Storyteller Bedtime Book* and *The Lion Storyteller
Book of Animal Tales*

A catalogue record for this book is available
from the British Library

Typeset in 15/23 Baskerville MT Schlbk
Printed and bound in Great Britain
by Cox and Wyman Ltd, Reading

Contents

The Very Strong Sparrow

'Too-tweet! Too-tweet! Too-tweet!' the baby birds cried out for their mother.

'Patience, patience,' said Sparrow. 'I've got food enough for everyone here.' And she fed them and hugged them, then wrapped her wings around them. And soon they were fast asleep.

KA-THOOM! KA-THOOM! KA-THOOM!

Elephant came tramping through the jungle. The earth shook. The trees shook. And so did poor Sparrow's nest.

'Too-tweet! Too-tweet! Too-tweet!' cried the baby birds. They were startled, and frightened, and wide awake!

Sparrow was furious. 'See what you've done!' she complained to Elephant. 'You

woke up my babies with your tramping and your tromping and your trumpeting. Could you try to be a little quieter?'

KA-THOOM! KA-THOOM! KA-THOOM!

Elephant tramped over to Sparrow's tree.

'Who do you think you're talking to?' he demanded. 'You are nothing but a tiny little sparrow. I am Elephant – the strongest animal in the jungle. And I will do whatever I please.'

'The strongest animal in the jungle? I don't believe it,' said Sparrow. And then, without thinking, she added, 'Why, even I could beat a big bully like you.'

Elephant tossed his trunk in the air and gave a trumpet blast. He had never been so insulted. 'Meet me tomorrow at noon, at the old banana tree,' he roared. 'We will have a test of strength and see who is the strongest animal in the jungle.' Then he tramped away, angry. KA-THOOM! KA-THOOM! KA-THOOM!

What have I done? thought Sparrow. Well, I had to do something. He was waking up my babies, after all.

Later that day, Sparrow flew to the river to take a bath and to fetch some water for her children. But just as she landed at the water's edge, Crocodile appeared.

KER-SPLASH! KER-SPLASH! KER-SPLASH!

He thrashed his scaly tail back and forth across the water till Sparrow thought she was going to drown.

'Stop it!' she cried. 'All I want is a little

water for myself and my babies.'

'Who do you think you are talking to?' snapped Crocodile. 'You are nothing but a tiny little sparrow. I am Crocodile – the strongest animal in the jungle. And I will do whatever I please.'

Sparrow had heard this before and she was about to fly away, when she had an idea.

'The strongest animal in the jungle?' she laughed. 'I don't believe it. I will meet you here, tomorrow, just after noon. And I will

show you that I am more powerful than you
can ever hope to be.'

Crocodile laughed so hard, there were
tears in his eyes.

'I'll take you up on that,' he chuckled.
'And if you win, you may drink from my
river whenever you like.'

The next day, as the sun reached the top
of the sky, Sparrow met Elephant by the old
banana tree. She had the end of a long,
thick vine in her beak.

'For our test of strength,' she said, 'we

shall have a tug of war.

You hold this end

of the vine,

and I will fly

off and grab

hold of the

other end. And when I cry "Pull!" we shall see who is the strongest.'

KA-THOOM! KA-THOOM! KA-THOOM!

Elephant tramped up and down with joy. He could win this contest easily! So he took the vine from Sparrow and she flew off to grab the other end.

But when she picked up the other end, she did not cry 'Pull!'. At least, not straight away. No, she carried the vine to the river, where Crocodile was waiting.

KER-SPLASH! KER-SPLASH! KER-SPLASH!

'So you've come after all,' he sneered.

'Yes,' she said. 'And I've come to win! We shall have a tug of war. You take this end, and I will fly off and grab the other end.

And when I cry "Pull!" we shall see who is
the strongest.'

Crocodile chuckled and clamped his teeth
onto the end of the vine. Then Sparrow
flew to the middle of the vine – to a spot
where she could hear both Elephant and
Crocodile, but where they could not hear
each other. And that's when she cried,
'PULL!'

KA-THOOM! KA-THOOM!
KA-THOOM!

Elephant pulled – feet stomping, neck straining, trunk swinging up and down.

KER-SPLASH! KER-SPLASH!
KER-SPLASH!

Crocodile pulled as well – feet splashing, teeth gnashing, tail thrashing back and forth.

They pulled for an hour. They pulled for two. But, pull as they might, neither could budge the other. At last, Elephant called through his aching teeth, 'Sparrow, I give up! I never would have believed it, but you are every bit as strong as I am. From now on I will tiptoe quietly past your tree.'

Crocodile called out as well. 'You win, mighty Sparrow. From now on, you may drink from my river whenever you like.'

So Sparrow went home to her little nest. And when she told her babies what she had done, they laughed and clapped their wings and cheered, 'Too-tweet! Too-tweet! Too-tweet!' For their mother was now the strongest animal in the jungle!

The Generous Rabbit

Rabbit shivered.

Rabbit sneezed.

The snow rose up to Rabbit's nose.

Rabbit rubbed her empty belly. Rabbit was hungry and tired and cold.

Then Rabbit stumbled across two turnips near the trunk of a tall pine tree.

So she hopped for joy, picked up the turnips and carried them all the way home.

Rabbit gobbled up the first turnip. But
when she got to the second, she was full.

I bet my friend Donkey could use this
turnip, Rabbit thought.

So she hopped all the way to Donkey's
house, and because Donkey was not at
home, she left the turnip in Donkey's dish.

Donkey was looking for food as well.

Donkey shivered.

Donkey sneezed.

The snow rose up to Donkey's knees.

Donkey rubbed his empty belly. He was tired and hungry and cold.

Then Donkey spied two potatoes, near a fence in the farmer's field.

So he gave a happy 'hee-haw', picked up the potatoes and carried them home.

Donkey gobbled up both potatoes, and then he noticed that a turnip had mysteriously appeared in his dish.

Now how did that get there? Donkey wondered. And being much too full to eat it, Donkey thought of his friend Sheep.

So Donkey carried the turnip to Sheep's house, and because Sheep was not at home, Donkey left the turnip on Sheep's soft bed of straw.

Sheep was looking for food as well.

Sheep shivered.

Sheep sneezed.

The snow rose up to Sheep's woolly tail.

Sheep rubbed her empty belly. She was tired and hungry and cold.

Then Sheep spotted a cabbage in the shadow of a snow-covered bush.

So she bleated a happy 'Hooray!' and picked up the cabbage and carried it home.

Sheep gobbled up the cabbage. And then she noticed that a turnip had mysteriously appeared on her bed.

Now how did that get there? Sheep wondered. And, being much too full to eat it, she thought of her friend Squirrel.

So Sheep carried the turnip to Squirrel's house. And because Squirrel was not at

home, she shoved the turnip into Squirrel's
tree-trunk hole.

Squirrel was looking for food as well. (Just
like everyone else!)

Squirrel shivered.

Squirrel sneezed.

The snow rose right up to Squirrel's ears.

Squirrel rubbed his empty belly. He was
tired and hungry and cold.

And then Squirrel sniffed out a few nuts

buried deep in the snowy soil.

Squirrel was so excited that he shook his bushy tail.

Then he carried the nuts back to his house.

When he got there, however, he couldn't get in. Someone had shoved a turnip into his tree-trunk hole!

Now how did that get there? Squirrel wondered. And as he gobbled up the nuts, he thought of a friend, a friend who could surely use something to eat.

So he pulled the turnip out of the hole and pushed it through the snow, all the way... to Rabbit's house!

Rabbit was asleep, so Squirrel left the turnip by her side and crept quietly back home.

When Rabbit awoke, she was no longer

tired, she was no longer cold. But she was
hungry again.

I wish I'd kept that extra turnip, she
thought. And when she opened her eyes,
there it was, right beside her!

Now how did that get here? Rabbit
wondered. Then she gobbled it up until she
was full.

Tortoise Brings Food

The sun was hot. The earth was dry. There had been no rain for many months. And now there was no food. The animals were very hungry.

Lion, king of all the beasts, called his thin and tired friends together under the shade of a tall, gnarled tree.

'The legends say this is a special tree,' he roared, 'which will give us all the food we

need – if only we can say its secret name.
But there is only one person who knows that
name – the old man who lives at the top of
the mountain.'

'Then we must go to him,' trumpeted
Elephant, 'as quickly as we can! Before we
all starve to death.'

'I'll go,' said Tortoise slowly. And
everyone just stopped and stared.

'Don't be silly,' roared Lion. 'It would
take you for ever! No, we shall send Hare
to find the name of the tree. He will be
back in no time.'

Hare hurried up the side of the mountain,
his long ears blown back against the side
of his head. He leaped. He scampered.
He raced. And soon he was face to face
with the old man.

'Please tell me the name of the special tree,' he begged. 'The animals are very hungry.'

The old man looked. The old man listened. And then the old man said one word and one word only: 'Unwungelema.'

'Thank you,' panted Hare. And then he hurried back down the mountainside.

He leaped. He scampered. He raced. All the while repeating to himself the name of the special tree: 'Uwungelema,  Uwungelema, Uwungelema.' But just as he reached the bottom of the mountain, Hare hurried

– CRASH! – right into the side of a huge anthill, and knocked himself silly.

So silly, in fact, that by the time he had staggered back to all the other animals, he had completely forgotten the name of the special tree!

'We must send someone else,' roared Lion. 'Someone who will not forget.'

'I'll go,' said Tortoise again.

And this time, the other animals laughed.

'We'll have starved to death by the time you get back,' chuckled Lion. 'No, we shall send Elephant.'

Elephant hurried up the side of the mountain, his long trunk swaying back and forth. He tramped. He trundled. He tromped. And soon he was face to face with the old man.

'Please tell me the name of the special tree,' he begged. 'The animals are very hungry.'

The old man looked puzzled. 'I have already told Hare,' he said. 'But I suppose I can tell you too.' And then he said that word: 'Uwungelema.'

'Thank you,' panted Elephant. And then he hurried back down the mountainside.

He tramped. He trundled. He tromped. All the while repeating to himself that secret name: 'Uwungelema, Uwungelema, Uwungelema.'

But, just like Hare, he was in such a hurry that he failed to notice the anthill. And he stumbled – CRASH! – right into its side, knocking himself so silly that he, too, forgot the secret name.

'This is ridiculous!' roared Lion. 'Is there no one who can remember a simple name?'

'I can,' said Tortoise quietly.

And the other animals just shook their heads.

'Enough!' roared Lion. 'It looks as if I shall have to do this myself.'

So Lion hurried up the hill and talked to the old man. But on the way back he, too, stumbled into the anthill and staggered back to the others, having forgotten the name completely.

'What shall we do now?' moaned Giraffe.

'I will go,' said Tortoise, determined to help. And before anyone could say anything, he started up the mountain.

He did not hurry, for that is not the tortoise way. Instead, he toddled. He trudged. He took one small step at a time. And, finally, he reached the old man.

'Please tell me the name of the special tree,' he said slowly, 'for my friends are very hungry.'

The old man looked angrily at Tortoise. 'I have already given the name to Hare, to Elephant and to Lion. I will say it one more time. But if you cannot remember it, I will not say it again!'

And then he spoke the word: 'Uwungelema.'

'Thank you,' said Tortoise, as politely
as he could. 'I promise you that I will not
forget.' And he started back down the
mountain.

He toddled. He trudged. He took one
small step at a time, all the while slowly
repeating, 'Uwungelema, Uwungelema,
Uwungelema.' And when he came to the
anthill, he simply wandered round it. For
he was in no hurry. No hurry at all.

When he returned, the animals huddled
round him.

'Do you know the name?' they asked.
'Did you remember it?'

'Of course,' Tortoise smiled. 'It's not hard
at all.' Then he looked at the special tree
and said the word: 'Uwungelema.'

Immediately, sweet, ripe fruit burst out from the special tree's branches and fell to the ground before the hungry animals. They hollered. They cheered. They ate till they were full – that day and the next and all through the terrible famine.

And, when the famine was over, they made Tortoise their new king. And they never laughed at him again.

The Determined Frog

Splish and splash. Jump and croak. Frog hopped in and out of the muddy pond.

His mother was there. His father too. And all twenty-seven brothers and sisters – diving and swimming and paddling about.

'There must be more to life than this muddy pond,' Frog said to himself one day.

So, splish and splash, jump and croak,

he hopped away from the pond and across the farmyard.

He passed the pen where the pigs lay and the little hut where the chickens clucked. And came, at last, to the barn.

Now this is interesting, he thought. And Frog hopped inside.

The barn was huge! The barn was empty! So he spent the whole day hopping – from here to hay, and hay to there. And as the sun slipped beneath the window sills and sent the shadows lengthening, Frog took one last, long leap – and landed, KERPLUNK, in a pitcher of cream!

Splish and splash. Jump and croak.

Oh dear, thought Frog. This is the strangest water I ever swam in. And the slipperiest too!

Frog tried to climb out of the pitcher, but he kept slipping back down the sides. And because the pitcher was so deep, he could not push his feet against the bottom and jump out either.

I'm stuck here! Frog realized at last. And then he croaked and croaked for help. But the barn was still empty. It was dark outside now. And his family was far away.

Splish and splash. Jump and croak.

Frog paddled and paddled, trying hard to keep his head above the cream. But he knew that, sooner or later, his strength would give out and he would slip to the bottom of the pitcher and drown.

So Frog thought and thought. He thought of his mother, and how he would miss her happy croaking in the morning.

'I can't give up and I won't give up!' Frog grunted to himself. And he paddled even harder.

Then Frog thought of his father, and how they would never again catch flies together with their long, sticky tongues.

'I can't give up and I won't give up!' Frog grunted again. And he paddled harder still.

Finally, Frog thought of his brothers and

sisters, and how he would miss playing hop-tag and web-tackle with them.

'I CAN'T GIVE UP AND I WON'T GIVE UP!' Frog grunted and shouted and groaned. Then he paddled as hard as he could.

And that's when Frog's feet felt something. The cream under his webbed toes was no longer wet and slippery. Instead, it was hard and lumpy. For with all his paddling, Frog had churned that cream into butter!

Frog rested his feet against the butter. He pushed hard with his strong back legs. And with a grunt and a shove, he leaped out of

the pitcher and onto the barn floor.

Then the frog who would not give up
hopped straight back home and lived
happily ever after – splishing and
splashing, jumping and croaking – with
his family in the muddy pond.

The Clever
Mouse Deer

The King of All Tigers in the Jungles of Java
called for his tiger friends.

'There is not enough meat in the Jungles
of Java!' the King of All Tigers roared.

'Not enough elephants.

'Not enough pigs.

'Not enough monkeys and apes.'

So the King of All Tigers in the Jungles of
Java pulled a whisker from his tiger face.

'Take this to the King of All Beasts in Borneo and tell him that we are coming.

'To eat up his elephants.

'To eat up his pigs.

'To eat up his monkeys and apes.'

'And if the King of All Beasts, all the beasts in Borneo, should try and stand in our way, then tell the King of All Beasts in Borneo that we will happily eat him up too!'

So the friends of the King of All Tigers in the Jungles of Java sailed across the sea.

And when they arrived on the shores of Borneo, what did the tigers find?

A Mouse Deer, that's all – a creature both frail and small.

'The King of All Tigers in the Jungles of Java has a message for your king. Give him

this whisker. Tell him we're coming –
coming to eat up his meat!'

The Mouse Deer ran off into the Jungles
of Borneo, wondering what to do.

For there was no King of All Beasts in
Borneo to give the message to!

The Mouse Deer was frail. The Mouse
Deer was small. But the Mouse Deer was
clever as well. So she went to her friend the

porcupine and asked her for one sharp quill.

'You're meat, and I'm meat!' the Mouse Deer explained. 'And the tigers will eat us both! But if you give me just one of your quills, I think I can make them go!'

So the Mouse Deer ran back through the Jungles of Borneo with the quill between her teeth.

When she got to the shores of Borneo, the tigers were there on the beach.

'So what's the answer?' roared the tigers of Java. 'What was your king's reply?'

'The answer is NO,' said the Mouse Deer, shaking as she laid the quill at their feet.

'The King of All Beasts – all the beasts in Borneo – gives you his whisker too. Take it back to your king. Tell him come, if he must. But we'll fight him, that's what we'll do!'

The tigers of Java stared at the quill.

They trembled at what they saw. If this was a whisker, then imagine the face to which that whisker belonged!

The whisker was huge, the whisker was pointy, the whisker was sharp and fierce!

The King of All Beasts, all the beasts in Borneo, must be some kind of monster, they guessed.

So the tigers of Java climbed back into
their boat and sailed home across the sea.

And when the King of All Tigers saw the
whisker, he changed his plans at once!

And that's why, today, in the Jungles of
Java, you may still hear a tiger's call.

But among the beasts, the beasts of
Borneo, there are no tigers at all!

The Noble Rooster

Rooster was never on time.

His job was simple enough, really.

Wake up early.

Watch for the sun.

And then cry 'Cock-a-doodle-do'.

But Rooster couldn't seem to get the hang of it.

He didn't like waking up early.

He fell asleep as he watched for the sun.

And that's why his 'Cock-a-doodle-dos' were always late.

The other chickens never let him forget it. They clucked and cackled and flapped their disapproval as he picked his way down from the barn roof each day.

And that's what he thought they were doing, one particularly bright and sunny morning.

'Sorry,' he muttered.

'Late again, I know,' he yawned.

'Won't happen next time,' he promised.

But no one paid any attention to him. And finally, he realized that they weren't talking about him at all.

'Haven't you heard?' clucked a big brown hen. 'The ogre who lives on top of the mountain has been stomping all over the farmer's crops! And he has told the farmer that he will stop only if the farmer promises to give him a chicken to eat, each and every day!'

'The farmer has challenged the ogre to a contest,' clucked a little yellow chick. 'If the ogre can build a stairway up the mountainside in just one night, the farmer will do what he asks. But if he cannot, the ogre will leave us all in peace.'

'And that's where you come in, Rooster,'

clucked a third chicken. 'The farmer and the ogre have agreed that the contest will come to an end when the sun rises and the rooster crows. We don't want the ogre to have any more time than necessary, which means that, for once, just once, you must not be late!'

Rooster wanted to say, 'I can't do it.'

He wanted to beg, 'Find someone else.'

He wanted to shout, 'No, anyone but me!'

But one look at the chickens convinced him. They were counting on him. And he was determined, this time, not to let them down.

That very night, as the sun fell behind the barn, the contest began. The chickens watched nervously as the ogre picked up the first stone step and put it in place. He was gruesome, grumpy and green. He had one horrible horn sticking out of the top of his head. And he was very, very strong. But it was a long way up the mountainside, so one by one all the hens dropped off to sleep.

Rooster, meanwhile, was hiding in a corner of the farmyard. He knew he could never wake up on time. He knew that everyone was counting on him. So he decided not to go to sleep at all. And that way, he would be sure to greet the rising sun.

He walked round and round.

He jumped up and down.

He sang little songs and played little games and splashed his face again and again with cold water. He kept himself so busy, in fact, that he did not notice when that clever ogre sneaked into the farmyard. He did not see when that clever ogre slipped

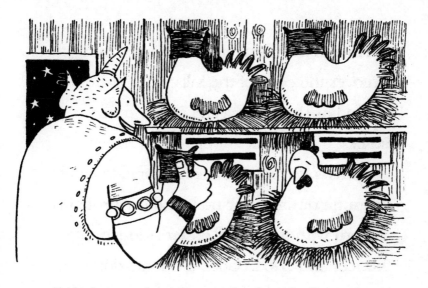

a little brown hood over the head of every
sleeping chicken. And he did not hear when
that clever ogre chuckled quietly to himself,
'Now there will be no one to crow at the
rising of the sun, and I'll be sure to win!'

But there was someone left to crow –
someone whose eyelids grew heavy, whose
head kept dropping on his feathery chest,
but who kept awake as the stone stairway
grew, step by step.

And as the first ray of morning sun crept up over the edge of the hills…

And as the ogre picked up the final stone…

And as he reared back his horrible head to laugh at his clever trick and celebrate his victory with a shout, Rooster staggered to his feet and cried, 'Cock-a-doodle-do!'

It was a sleepy cock-a-doodle-do.

And it was a quiet cock-a-doodle-do.

But it was a cock-a-doodle-do nonetheless.

A cock-a-doodle-do that woke the farmer and the chickens and made the ogre howl, 'Nooooo!'

The farmer was delighted.

The chickens were puzzled. Why is it still dark? they wondered.

And the ogre just dropped the last stone

and walked over the mountain, dejected –
never to be seen again.

There was a great celebration, of course.
In the farmhouse. And in the farmyard too!
And even though Rooster never again
managed to cry 'cock-a-doodle-do' on time,
no one ever complained. Because he had
done his best when it really mattered.

Why the Cat Falls
on Her Feet

Manabozho walked silently on two feet
through the forest. He spied Eagle soaring,
two wings wide above the tree tops. He
caught Spider skittering, eight feet dancing
through the fallen leaves. But he did not
hear his enemy, Snake, slithering on no feet
behind him more silently still.

'Manabozho thinks he is strong,' Snake
hissed to himself, 'because he walks tall on

his two feet. But when he tires, and when he lies down – level with me, on no feet at all – then we shall see who is the strongest!'

Manabozho walked all day. But when, at last, the sun wandered beneath the reach of Eagle's wings, and then beneath the treetops too, Manabozho leaned his spear against the trunk of an oak and lay down upon the ground.

He said goodnight to Ant, six legs struggling to carry a tiny seed. He winked at waking Possum, hanging one-tail from a nearby branch. But when Manabozho closed his eyes, Snake slipped silently to his side.

Snake reared back his head. Snake opened his mouth. Snake showed his sharp and poisonous fangs. But just as Snake was ready to strike, someone struck him from behind.

It was Cat, who had been hiding in the branches of the tall oak. Cat, who had seen what Snake was about to do and leaped, four feet flying, to stop him.

Cat landed on Snake's back and dug four sets of claws into his shiny skin. He turned to bite her, but she was too quick. Again

and again she leaped, claws flashing, screeching and scratching until Manabozho was awakened by her cries. He jumped to his feet, and reached for his spear. But by then, the battle was over. Snake was dead, and Cat stood trembling on her four feet beside him.

'Such bravery must be rewarded!' Manabozho declared. 'With your four feet, you have saved my life, and so from this time on, wherever you fall, you will always land on your feet – and those four feet will save *you* as well!'

The Clever Mouse

Many years ago, in a little Welsh town,
there was a famine. There was no food
anywhere. And everyone – from the richest
lord to the poorest peasant – was tired and
thin and hungry.

One day, a monk named Cadog came to
visit the town. Cadog was good and gentle
and kind. He loved God. He loved God's
creatures. And he loved to read and write

and learn. In fact, that was why he had come to the town – to study under a wise and famous teacher.

'You may be my student,' the teacher promised, 'but I must warn you. There is a famine in these parts, so I have nothing to feed you.'

Cadog didn't mind. Not one bit. He studied hard, day after day at his little desk. And every day he had a visitor – a tiny visitor with fine, grey whiskers, a pointed nose, and a long, pink tail. He climbed on Cadog's desk, and scurried across his books, and scampered over his pile of goose-quill pens.

But Cadog didn't mind. Not one bit. He liked the little mouse and refused to chase him away. And perhaps that is why, one day, the little mouse arrived with a gift.

He climbed onto Cadog's desk. He
scampered over Cadog's pens. And, in the
middle of Cadog's book, he dropped one
yellow grain of wheat!

'Thank you, my friend,' said Cadog to
the mouse.

And the mouse sat up and squeaked, as if
to say, 'You're welcome.'

Half an hour later he returned with another
piece of wheat and Cadog thanked him again.

Soon, the mouse returned a third time.
Then a fourth. And a fifth. And a sixth. And
when there were finally seven golden grains of
wheat lying on his book, Cadog had an idea.

He took a long piece of silken thread and
gently tied one end around the mouse's leg.

'This won't hurt at all,' he promised.
'And it may do a world of good.' Then he
let the mouse go and watched to see where
it would run. The mouse was much too fast
for Cadog, of course. But by following the
silken thread he was able to trace the
mouse's path – into a hole in the wall,
out the other side, across the
garden, through the
woods, and into a huge
earthen mound.

Cadog ran to fetch his teacher, and together they dug into the mound. Buried deep within were the ruins of an old house. And buried deep in the cellar of that old house was an enormous pile of wheat!

Cadog and his teacher ran to tell their friends. And soon the town was filled with the smell of freshly baked bread. Now there was plenty of food for everyone!

The next day, the little mouse came to visit as usual. He climbed onto Cadog's desk. He scampered over Cadog's pens. And when he sat down in the middle of Cadog's book, the monk gently untied the silken thread.

'Thank you, my friend,' he said. 'God sent you to me for a reason. And now we know what it was. Your keen nose and tiny feet have saved the entire town.'

Then he tore off a chunk of fresh, warm bread, and set it before the little creature. And the mouse and the monk shared a meal together.

A Note from the Author

As you may wish to read other versions of some of these traditional stories, I would like to acknowledge some of the sources I have referred to, although most of these stories can be found in several collections.

'The Very Strong Sparrow' from 'The Strongest Sparrow in the Forest' and 'Tortoise Brings Food' from 'Uwungelema' in *African Fairy Tales* by K. Arnott, Frederick Muller Ltd, London. 'The Generous Rabbit' from *The Rabbit and the Turnip*, tr. Richard Sadler, Doubleday and Company Inc., Garden City, New York, 1968. 'The Determined Frog' from 'The Wise Frog and the Foolish Frog' in *Tales from Central Russia* by J. Riordan, Kestrel Books, London. 'The Clever Mouse Deer' from *Indonesian Fairy Tales*; Adele deLeeuw, Frederick Muller Ltd, London. 'The Noble Rooster' from *Little One-Inch and Other Japanese Children's Favorite Stories*, ed. Florence Sakade, Charles E. Tuttle Company, Rutland, Vermont, 1984. 'Why the Cat Falls on Her Feet' from *The Folktale Cat*, Frank de Caro, Barnes and Noble Books, New York, 1992. 'The Clever Mouse' from 'St Cadog and the Mouse' in *Welsh Legendary Tales* by E. Sheppard-Jones, Nelson, Edinburgh.